218355

SPORTS CLINIC

Football:
Passing

By Stephen Holden

Children's Press
A Division of Grolier Publishing
New York / London / Hong Kong / Sydney
Danbury, Connecticut

A special thanks to Roselle High School in Roselle, New Jersey

Book Design: Nelson Sa
Contributing Editor: Rob Kirkpatrick

Photo Credits: Cover © Angelo Barros and Nelson Sa; p. 5 © Ezra Shaw/All Sport; p. 7 © Brian Bahr/All Sport; p. 8 © Eliot Schechter/All Sport; p. 11 © Angelo Barros and Nelson Sa; p. 12 © Jonathan Daniel/All Sport; pp. 17, 18 © Angelo Barros and Nelson Sa; p. 21 © Brian Bahr/All Sport; p. 22 © Andy Lyons/All Sport; pp. 24, 26, 27 © Angelo Barros and Nelson Sa; pp. 29, 30 © Ezra Shaw/All Sport; p. 34 © Angelo Barros and Nelson Sa; p. 37 © Ezra Shaw/All Sport; pp. 38, 41 © Angelo Barros and Nelson Sa.

Visit Children's Press on the Internet at:
http://publishing.grolier.com

Library of Congress Cataloging-in-Publication Data

Holden, Stephen, 1969-
   Football: Passing / by Stephen Holden.
    p. cm. – (Sports clinic)
   Includes bibliographical references and index.
   Summary: This book explains the basics of completing a pass play and the skills and prac-
      tice needed to become part of a high-powered passing offense.
   ISBN 0-516-23364-5 (lib. bdg.) – ISBN 0-516-23564-8 (pbk.)
   1. Passing (Football)—Juvenile literature. 2. Football—Offense—United States—Juvenile
literature. [1. Passing (Football) 2. Football.] I. Title. II. Series.

GV951.5.H65 2000
796.332'25—dc21
                                                                    00-026218

CONTENTS

INTRODUCTION

In football, the offense tries different plays to get into the other team's end zone. Sometimes, the offense will try to run the ball. Other times, the offense will try to move the ball downfield (toward the other team's end zone) by passing the ball.

When you think of passing, you might think only of the quarterback. However, the quarterback is one of eleven players on a team's offense. Each of the eleven players has a job to do on every play. If just one player does his job poorly, the whole play can break down.

This book will explain the basics of completing a pass play. If you learn the necessary skills and practice them over and over again, someday you might become part of a high-powered passing offense.

Ready . . . break!

A team with a good offense is an exciting thing to watch.

ONE

THE PLAYERS

There are eleven players on offense. Usually, these players consist of the quarterback, five offensive linemen, two wide receivers, a tight end, and two running backs. At the beginning of each play, the referee places the ball on the field. The ball placement sets the line of scrimmage. The scrimmage line marks where a play starts. When an offensive play moves the ball to another place on the field, that place becomes the new scrimmage line for the next play.

The offense must have at least seven players lined up next to one another on the line of scrimmage. These players make up the offensive line. By rule, only the two players on either end of the offensive line are allowed to catch a pass. Also, any player that lines up behind the scrimmage line is allowed to catch passes.

Every play begins with players at the scrimmage line.

THE QUARTERBACK

Every play for the offense begins with the quarter-back getting the ball from the center. The center, along with every other lineman, crouches down in a three-point stance (one hand and two feet on the ground). The center is in his stance with his "down" hand on the ball. The quarterback stands behind him. When the quarterback says "Hut!" the center hands the ball between his legs to the quarterback. This is called the snap.

The quarterback is the player who passes (throws) the ball to pass receivers. The quarterback must have a strong arm. He must be able to throw the ball far and with accuracy.

Making Decisions

The quarterback also must be a smart player who can make good decisions. He must be able to see receivers who are not being guarded too closely by defenders. A receiver that is far enough away from a defender is said to be "open." At this point, the

The quarterback gets the ball at
the beginning of every offensive play.

quarterback wants to pass the ball to the receiver. He does not want to throw the ball to a receiver who is not open. If he does, a player from the other team might intercept the pass.

The Leader

The quarterback is the leader of the offense. Before every play, the quarterback and the rest of the offense huddle (get together). In the huddle, the quarterback tells the offense what kind of play they will use.

OFFENSIVE LINEMEN

The seven offensive players who start every play at the line of scrimmage make up the offensive line. The five players in the middle of the line are the center, two guards, and two tackles. The linemen use a three-point stance. The center crouches over the ball. He snaps the ball to the quarterback. The center plays between two guards. The tackles line up on either end of the guards. These five players are called offensive linemen. The offensive linemen try to block (stop) the defense from tackling the quarterback.

Offensive linemen have to be big and strong.

10

The Players

Linemen must be big, strong, and heavy. They need to stop big defensive players from tackling the ball carrier. They do most of their blocking on the line of scrimmage. It is not important for linemen to be quick or to have good hands because they don't have to catch passes.

THE TIGHT END

The tight end stands on one end of the scrimmage line, next to one of the tackles. Because he lines up on the end of the scrimmage line, he is allowed to catch passes. He also has to block defenders. Tight ends need to be big and strong so that they can block. At the same time, they need to be quick. Their quickness allows them to be open to catch passes.

DID YOU KNOW?

By rule, National Football League (NFL) quarterbacks can wear only numbers 1 through 19. Running backs must wear numbers 20 through 49. Offensive linemen wear numbers between 60 and 79. Tight ends and wide receivers wear numbers 80 through 89.

A good tight end, such as Shannon Sharpe, can help his team with his strength and his speed.

13

WIDE RECEIVERS

Each offense has wide receivers (wideouts) whose main job it is to catch passes. Sometimes, they line up on the end of the offensive line. Other times, they line up a few feet behind the line and out toward the side-lines. Wide receivers need to be fast so that they can get open on passing plays. When they catch passes, they need speed to run away from defenders and toward the other team's end zone.

RUNNING BACKS

The quarterback is not the only player who starts each play in the backfield (behind the scrimmage line). The quarterback usually has one or two running backs with him. Running backs need to be quick so that they can run with the ball. They don't need to be huge, but they should be big enough so that they can block. They also need to have steady hands because they often carry the ball.

The main job of the wide receiver is to catch and run with the ball.

THROWING A PASS

Passing may sound simple. The quarterback throws the ball. The receiver catches it. Actually, it is a complicated process. There are many steps that players must learn before a team can complete a pass play.

TAKING THE SNAP

A quarterback must know how to take a snap from the center. When you come out of the offensive huddle, wait until the linemen crouch down in their stance. Stand directly behind the center. Bend at your knees and reach between the center's legs (See Figure 1). Your throwing hand should be on top and your other hand on the bottom. When the center snaps the ball, wrap your bottom hand around the ball.

Figure 1: Each offensive play begins with a snap from center.

THE GRIP

Quarterbacks' grips vary from player to player based on the size of their hands. Generally, you should place your fingers over the top of the laces. Place your pinky and ring finger firmly against the ball. Put the tip of your middle finger above the laces. Spread your index finger toward the end of the ball, with the fingertip on the seam of the football. The thumb should be as far around the other side of the ball as possible (See Figure 2). Your palm should hold the football just away from the ball's center.

Your nonthrowing hand should hold the under-side of the ball. This hand helps you to keep a steady grip on the ball.

DROPPING BACK

The defense will try to tackle you before you can throw the ball. After the snap, you need to drop back (step away) from the scrimmage line. The drop gives you extra time to throw the ball.

To drop back, take your first step with the foot on your throwing side. Then, cross over with your other foot. Take a few steps back. As you drop back, you should hold the ball at chest height. This gets your hands ready to throw a pass.

The number of steps you take when you drop back will vary according to the type of pass play. It also can depend on your coach. Different coaches may prefer to use different drops. Drops can be three, five, or seven steps. To throw a quick pass, a quarter-back might use a three-step drop. For long passes, he can use a seven-step drop. This drop buys the quarterback more time while receivers run downfield.

Figure 2: A good pass begins with a good grip.

THROWING THE BALL

Once you drop back, you can begin your throwing motion. There are four steps to throwing a football: getting set, stepping forward, delivering the ball, and following through.

Getting Set

The last step of the drop back is also your "set" step. As you take this last step, plant your foot firmly. This step stops your backward motion and helps you to control your body.

Stepping Forward

Step forward with the foot opposite your throwing hand. Step toward your target. As you step forward, take your nonthrowing hand off the football and bring back your throwing hand. It should come up to ear level and go behind your head.

Kurt Warner keeps his elbow bent as his arm comes forward for the pass.

Throwing a Pass

Delivering the Ball

Turn your hips so that your body faces your target. As you open your hips, your upper body will follow. The shoulder of your throwing arm will come forward. Keep your elbow bent as your arm comes forward. Then, as your arm straightens out, release the ball from your hand.

DID YOU KNOW?

The quarterback rarely throws a ball directly to the receiver. The quarterback must time his pass so that it will arrive at the spot where the receiver is running. This is called leading the receiver.

As you release, your fingers should roll off the ball. Your middle finger should be the last one to release the ball. By rolling your fingers, you put a spin on the ball. A perfect pass will spin tightly. This type of pass is called a spiral. A spiral pass travels farther in the air. It also does not wobble, so it is easier to catch.

Following Through

After you have released the ball, your forearm should extend and be pointing toward your target. Your throwing hand should be angled toward the center of your body (See Figure 3).

Figure 3: A good passing motion results in a smooth follow-through.

RECEIVING A PASS

Catching a football is a skill that you must learn. Even the best NFL receivers need to practice catching the ball. They also need to know how to run patterns (paths) that help them to get open.

GETTING OPEN

It's almost impossible for you to catch a pass unless you open. To keep you from running your pattern, a defender may try to bump or grab you at the line of scrimmage. You need to be able to shed (get away from) this defender. When the ball is snapped, take a step toward the defender. Then, angle to the left or right of the defender, depending on the pattern you have to run. If the defender tries to bump you, swing up your closest arm to swat him away.

Pass receiving is a skill that requires a lot of practice.

25

A good receiver knows how to release from (get quickly past) the scrimmage line. Once he releases from the scrimmage line, he can run downfield, complete his pattern, and get open.

HOW TO CATCH THE BALL

To catch a pass, hold out your hands and move them to meet the ball. You should be able to see the ball land in your hands. Cushion the ball with your throwing hand and trap it with your other hand.

Above the Numbers

If the pass is at or above chest level, place the thumbs and index fingers of your hands together. They should form a triangle where the nose of the ball goes. Make sure your palms face the ball, not the ground (See Figure 4).

Figure 4: This is the proper way to catch a ball at chest level.

Receiving a Pass

Below the Numbers

You hold your hands differently to catch a ball below chest level. Place your little fingers together. In this position, your hands form a basket.

Over the Shoulder

If you have to catch a ball over your shoulder, hold your two hands up with the two little fingers touching. Keep your fingers spread.

Away from the Body

Many young receivers make the mistake of trying to trap the ball against their bodies. This actually makes it harder to catch the ball. The ball can bounce off your body or your uniform's padding. To catch a football, meet the ball with your hands and bring it toward your body (See Figure 5).

Figure 5: You should catch the ball with your hands away from your body.

DID YOU KNOW?

The clock stops every time the quarterback throws an incomplete pass. If time is running out on the game clock, the quarterback might take a quick one-step drop and throw a pass into the ground. This gives his team more time to score points before the end of the game.

RUNNING AFTER THE CATCH

When you catch a pass, you should brace yourself for getting hit by a defender. Bring the ball into your body immediately. Tuck it between your arm and your midsection. You also may want to wrap your other forearm around the ball to keep it away from defenders.

Once you have the ball, try to run as far as you can toward the defense's end zone. If the game clock is winding down, you may want to run out of bounds just before you get tackled. When the ball carrier runs out of bounds, the referee stops the game clock. The clock doesn't start again until the next play begins.

Receivers can gain valuable yards for their team by running after the catch.

FOUR

PLAYS AND FORMATIONS

If you play in a pickup game with your friends, passing strategy is simple. The quarterback tells his receivers where to run. The receivers try to get open. The quarterback passes the ball to one of them.

In organized games, passing is much more complicated. The offense uses different lineups for different game situations. These lineups are called formations.

PASSING FORMATIONS

To complete a pass, every player in the formation must know what to do during the play. Even players on the sidelines have to pay attention. When the coach changes formations between plays, some

The offense lines up differently depending on the play that they will run.

players come off the field. New players go on to replace them. The coach changes formations to give his team the best chance to complete the game's next play.

Pro Set

The pro set is the most common formation in the NFL. In this formation, there are two wide receivers and one tight end. One wide receiver stands next to a tackle on the line of scrimmage. The other wide receiver lines up behind the line of scrimmage. There are two running backs in the backfield. They play behind the quarterback, on either side of him. In this formation, the running backs are in a good position either to block or to run and catch a short pass.

Three Wide Receivers

When a team switches from a pro set to a three-receiver formation, it sends one of its running backs off the field. Then, a substitute player from the sidelines goes on the field to play wide receiver. The remaining running back stands directly behind the quarterback. Teams like to use the three-wide-receiver formation because it gets their three best pass-catchers on the field. It also keeps a tight end and running back on the field for blocking or receiving.

Four Wide Receivers

In a four-wide-receiver formation, the tight end and one running back go off the field, and two more wide receivers come onto the field. The team puts two wide receivers on the offensive line—one on each end. The other two receivers stand out wide but behind the scrimmage line. This formation gets the four fastest pass receivers on the field.

Five Wide Receivers (Empty Backfield)

Sometimes, a team will want to give itself as many options as possible to complete a pass. The offense sends off its tight end and both running backs, and three more wide receivers come onto the field. The offense puts one wide receiver on each end of the offensive line. The team puts three more receivers out wide, just behind the line. Then, after the snap, the quarterback tries to find an open receiver as quickly as possible. He needs to find one fast because he doesn't have anyone in the backfield to block for him.

PASSING PLAYS

In the huddle, the quarterback tells his teammates what kind of passing or running play they will do. Good players will memorize all the plays that the

offense uses. When the quarterback calls the play, each player should know what to do on the play.

SHORT PASSES

Every team should know how to complete short pass plays. A short-distance pass might not move the ball very far downfield. However, short passes are easy for an offense to complete. The offense has up to four plays to move the ball 10 yards downfield. This is called getting a first down. As long as the offense gets first downs, they get to keep the ball. Short passes can be a great way for the offense to make first downs.

MEDIUM PASSES

Every great passing offense knows how to run medium-pass plays. A team can get about 10 or 15 yards if they complete a medium pass. Passes in this range are more difficult to complete than are short passes. The farther the quarterback has to throw a football, the less accuracy he will have.

In the huddle, the quarterback tells the offense what kind of pass they will attempt.

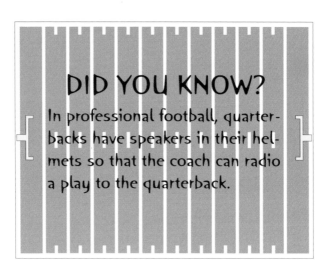

DID YOU KNOW?

In professional football, quarterbacks have speakers in their helmets so that the coach can radio a play to the quarterback.

DEEP PASSES

Sometimes, teams need to get downfield quickly. Or they might just want to gamble and go for a long pass play. In these situations, teams use deep passes. Deep-pass plays can be hard to complete. The quarterback has to lead the receiver in just the right way. But a team that can complete deep passes can score points quickly. An offense can move the ball more than twenty yards at once with a deep pass.

MULTIPLE RECEIVERS

On most passes, the quarterback will be able to choose from two or more receivers. In passing plays, receivers are given different pass patterns to run. Or

Deep-pass plays can score points quickly for the offense.

they might run the same patterns on opposite sides of the field. The quarterback will look for his first choice of receivers to see if he is open. This is called the primary receiver. If the primary receiver is not open, the quarterback will look to pass to another receiver.

DRILLS

No team, no matter how talented, can complete pass plays without practicing. Every player must practice his job over and over before he can compete in a real game. The following drills can help you to develop the skills you need to pass and catch a football:

Drop Back and Throw

Have a friend stand at different places on the field to catch a pass. Practice dropping back. Do a three-, five-, and seven-step drop. Once you are comfortable with each drop, practice throwing to your friend.

Hook-Pass Drill

This drill lets both the quarterback and wide receiver practice timing. The quarterback gets to practice leading the receiver with his throw. The receiver gets to practice running to catch the football. Practice a

A good quarterback spends a lot of time practicing passes.

five-step drop. Have the receiver run downfield. The distance depends on the quarterback's arm strength. As the receiver stops, the quarterback should throw the ball. The receiver should have to come back for it. This helps the receiver put space between himself and the defender. Try to throw the ball right at the receiver's chest.

Wide-Receiver Release

It is important for a wide receiver to get a good release from the defender at the beginning of a pass play. Stand on an imaginary line of scrimmage, opposite a defender. Have someone else stand several yards downfield. Have this person point left or right to tell you in which direction to run. Then, have the person tell you when to start. Pretend you are running a pass route. Try to get past the defender.

Hand Position

Stand 10 yards away from someone. Have that person call out a height and the placement of an imaginary

Passing drills help both the passer and the receiver.

pass. The height levels are: high (above your helmet), pads (at your shoulders), numbers (at your chest), belt (at your waist), and low (below your waist). The placements can be left, center, or right. This makes fifteen possible locations for the pass. When the person calls out a location, move your hands into position as quickly as possible. Remember: You want to reach away from your body.

KEEP PRACTICING

NFL stars such as John Elway, Brett Favre, Jerry Rice, and Randy Moss have shown fans many exciting pass plays. Each one of these stars started out as a young player who had to learn the basics of passing. Once you have learned the basics, you too might become a great football player!

NEW WORDS

backfield the area behind the line of scrimmage

block to push a defender away from the ball carrier

downfield toward the other team's end zone

drop when the quarterback steps away from the center after the snap

first down when the offense moves the ball at least ten yards downfield in no more than four plays

formation how the players line up on the field

huddle when the quarterback gets together with the offense and calls the next play

lead the receiver to throw the ball to the spot on the field to where the receiver is running

line of scrimmage an imaginary line from one sideline to the other that shows where a play begins

NEW WORDS

open when a receiver is far enough away from defenders to catch a pass

out of bounds off the field of play

pattern the path a receiver runs to get open for a pass

release from get past the defender at the line of scrimmage

shed a defender to get away from a defender

snap when the center gives the ball to the quarterback

three-point stance when a lineman crouches with one hand down on the ground before the snap

FOR FURTHER READING

Allen, James. *Football, Play Like A Pro*. Mahwah, NJ: Troll Communications L.L.C., 1990.

Bass, Tom. *Play Football the NFL Way: Position-by-Position Techniques and Drills for Offense, Defense, and Special Teams*. New York: St. Martin's Griffin, 1990.

Simms, Phil, Rick Meiser, and Jim Fassel. *Phil Simms on Passing: Fundamentals of Throwing the Football*. New York: William Morrow and Company, Incorporated, 1996.

Sullivan, George. *All About Football*. New York: The Putnam Publishing Group, 1990.

RESOURCES

Football Drills

Web site: *www.footballdrills.com*

This site includes drills for every position, including passing drills for the quarterback.

NFL.Com

Web site: *www.nfl.com*

This is the official site of the National Football League. It includes Web pages on teams, players, coaches, and many other parts of the game.

Pop Warner Football

Web site: *www.tdclub.com/ysnim/home/index.jsp*

This online center contains information about Pop Warner, the youth football league. It also has links to games, comics, and news about football.

RESOURCES

The Zone

Web site: *www.sportscombine.com/thezone/Drills/drills.htm*

Contains a list of drills for all positions. Read the drills submitted by others, or submit your own.

INDEX

INDEX

ABOUT THE AUTHOR

Stephen Holden is an avid, lifelong football fan. Steve's favorite position is fullback. He learned his love of football from his father, who was a star high school and college football player. Steve's favorite teams are the Syracuse Orangemen and the New York Giants. Steve's all-time favorite quarterback is Phil Simms.